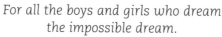

*For all the boys and girls who dream
the impossible dream.*
—COS

For my brother Tom—the born performer
—Jack Heath

For my water-babies, Eva, Jesse & Heath
—James Hart

First American Edition 2019
Kane Miller, A Division of EDC Publishing

Text & illustrations copyright © Scholastic Australia, 2018

Text by Cosentino with Jack Heath
Illustrations by James Hart
Published by Scholastic Australia in 2018
Internal images: p14 and various pages, Stars © Alisovna/Creative Market

For information contact:
Kane Miller, A Division of EDC Publishing
PO Box 470663
Tulsa, OK 74147-0663
www.kanemiller.com
www.edcpub.com
www.usbornebooksandmore.com

Library of Congress Control Number: 2018942377

Manufactured by Regent Publishing Services, Hong Kong
Printed January 2019 in ShenZhen, Guangdong, China

1 2 3 4 5 6 7 8 9 10

ISBN: 978-1-61067-980-0

THE MYSTERIOUS WORLD OF COSENTINO

THE LOST TREASURE

By COSENTINO

THE GRAND ILLUSIONIST

WITH JACK HEATH

ILLUSTRATED BY JAMES HART

Kane Miller
A DIVISION OF EDC PUBLISHING

THE MYSTERIOUS WORLD OF COSENTINO

COPPERTOWN/THE OCEAN

COSENTINO

MAGICIAN AT COPPERPOT THEATER
ABILITIES: ESCAPE, SLEIGHT OF HAND,
TELEKINESIS, ILLUSION

LOCKI

COS'S PARTNER AT COPPERPOT THEATER
ABILITIES: LOCK-PICKING

NONNA

PROP/COSTUME DESIGNER
COPPERFIELD COTTAGE
ABILITIES: HEALING POWERS

CAPTAIN ANCHOR

CAPTAIN OF SUNKEN OIL RIG, THE OCEAN
ABILITIES: VERY HEAVY,
CRYING UNDERWATER

KATALIN

OCEAN PROTECTOR
ABILITIES: MOST MAGICAL OCEAN CREATURE,
CAN BECOME INVISIBLE

BARRY AND STUART

KILLER WHALES
ABILITIES: CAN EAT ANYTHING,
HIGHLY LITERAL

THE MYSTERIOUS WORLD OF COSENTINO

SILVER CITY

HOLLOW

King's Henchman
Abilities: Can smell magic

THE KING OF DIAMONDS

King of Magicland
Abilities: Hypnotism

FLEX

King's Bodyguard
Abilities: Superstrong

PRINCESS PRISCILLA

Princess of Magicland
Abilities: Levitation, sweet, kind heart, extremely clever

LINK

King's Builder
Silver Castle, Silver City
Abilities: Unbreakable Grip

THE RIG

THE PIER

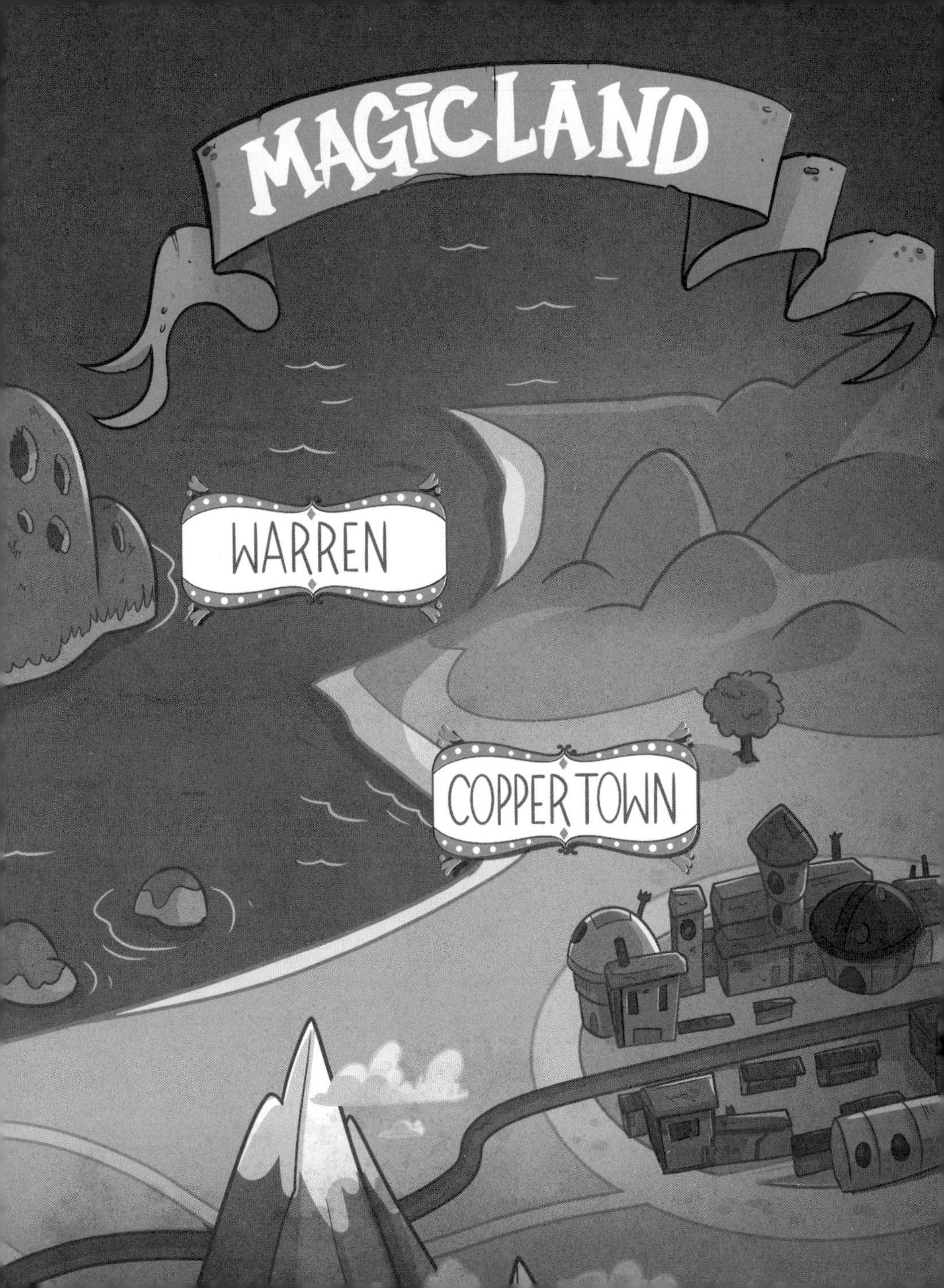
MAGIC LAND
WARREN
COPPERTOWN

Are You Watching Closely?

"Ladies and gentlemen," Cosentino said. "Are you watching closely?"

Everyone was. The pier was covered with audience members, all staring at Cos— and at the giant glass ball dangling from the crane. The small wooden grate on one side seemed to stare back, like an evil eye.

"I will be tied up, sealed in the glass ball and lowered into the ocean," Cos explained. "The ball

60 SECONDS

tick tick tick

will fill with water as the crane lowers it deeper and deeper into the sea. After sixty seconds, the water will be **over my head**.

"I'll have to escape from shackles and a straitjacket, pick two padlocks on the grate and swim up to the surface before I run out of air."

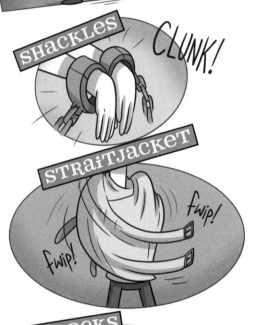

SHACKLES — CLUNK!

STRAITJACKET — fwip! fwip!

PADLOCKS — CLICK!

BREATHE!

10

Priscilla and Locki looked worried. Locki was probably just acting—he was Cos's best friend and had seen the Grand Illusionist escape from situations like this thousands of times. But this was the first time Priscilla would see it outside of rehearsals.

Cos winked at her. Priscilla didn't look reassured.

"I am an illusionist," Cos continued, "but this is not an illusion. I will be **suspended** just under the surface of the water. You will be able to see absolutely everything that happens inside the clear glass ball. Wish me **luck**."

He pulled a spray can from his pocket and painted some words on the side of the crane, just in case anyone at the back of the crowd hadn't heard what he said.

1 PAIR OF SHACKLES
1 STRAITJACKET
2 PADLOCKS
60 SECONDS OF AIR

When everyone had finished reading the words, Cos held up the spray can . . . Then he pushed it into his mouth and swallowed it.

The crowd's eyes went wide. A few people looked nervously over their shoulders. Magic was illegal in Coppertown. But this wasn't real magic—it was an illusion.

MAGIC SECRET UNLOCKED

While the audience was reading the words,
Cos had swapped the real spray can for a
fake one made of edible cardboard.

Cos licked his lips. "Yum. Bring me the
straitjacket!"

Locki stepped forward holding a strange coat
covered in buckles and straps.

"You're not going to eat it, are you?" he asked.

No one laughed. Everyone was staring fearfully
at the coat. The evil two-headed King sometimes
sent his army into Coppertown, looking for spell
books. His enforcer, Hollow, followed the trail of
spelldust to the forbidden books, arrested the
owners, and dragged them away in straitjackets
just like this.

Cos himself had an illegal spell book hidden away. He'd borrowed it from the library as a little kid and kept it when the King banned magic.

Everyone was on tiptoes, peering at the menacing glass ball. Some people were peering over the edge of the rail, looking down at the water. There were rumors of strange, hungry creatures under the sea. Sometimes scuba divers went down there and never came back. It was considered dangerous to go in the water even without being tied up.

Cos pulled the straitjacket over his head and pushed his arms into the sleeves. It was as tight as a car seat with twenty seat belts. When he stepped up onto the rail at the edge of the pier, he pretended to wobble in the wind. The crowd gulped.

Priscilla pulled on a thick rope, drawing the glass ball closer to the pier. She opened the grate so Cos could climb in. It wasn't quite big enough inside for him to stand up. The glass distorted the faces in the crowd.

I hope you know what you're doing.

Thanks for the encouragement!

Priscilla locked the grate with two big padlocks.
A few people came from the audience to rattle
the padlocks and check that they were real. When
they were satisfied, Priscilla released the rope.

The glass ball swung out over the dark ocean,
spinning in the breeze, dangling from the crane.
The movement made Cos dizzy. If he'd known

the weather would be this bad, he might have postponed the performance. Cos preferred to do these kinds of stunts inside a theater, where the wind didn't matter. Unfortunately, his old theater had burned down. His friends were helping him build a new one, but it wouldn't be ready for weeks. The people of Coppertown needed magic. Cos wasn't going to let them down.

AND THEN DISASTER STRUCK.

THE MIGHTY MAGNET

A trumpet blasted. Everyone turned to see
the King floating toward the pier on his magic
throne. His bodyguard, Flex, stomped along
beside him. A dozen mind-controlled soldiers
followed, along with Link, the King's builder.
Link was using her incredible strength to carry a
block of iron.

"Make way for his majesty, the King of
Diamonds!" Link cried.

The terrified crowd fled in every direction.
They didn't know why the King had
chosen to visit Coppertown that day,
but they weren't going to
wait and find out.
Within seconds, the
pier was empty.

The King's voice echoed across the space. "That was quick. Good work, Link. Who knew this was such a popular place!"

Cos could hear footsteps getting closer. When the King and his entourage passed the stack of crates, they would see Cos and Locki—known magic users who were to be **arrested** on sight.

Cos couldn't run away. He was **trapped** in shackles, a straitjacket and a glass ball. But he couldn't let the others get caught.

RUN! Quick!

What about you?

I'll be fine. Go!

Locki didn't move. He had rehearsed this escape with Cos hundreds of times. He knew it would take Cos **at least** two minutes to **escape** from the shackles, straitjacket and ball. The King would be here any second.

"I'll stall him," Priscilla said.

"Priscilla, no!" Cos cried. But it was too late. Priscilla **ran** past the stack of crates, and was quickly out of sight.

Locki spotted one of the hammers they had used to nail the equipment crates shut. He snatched it up, ready to smash the glass ball.

With the shackles around his ankles, Cos would sink to the bottom of the ocean. "I have a better idea."

Meanwhile, the King and his attendants were nearing the stack of crates when Priscilla came out from behind them.

"I say," the King said. "Is that my niece?"

"How should I know?" his other head complained. "Your newspaper is blocking my view."

Priscilla forced a smile. "Uncle! What a nice surprise."

"Priscilla," the King said. "What mischief are you up to now?"

"Mischief?" Priscilla asked innocently.

Mischief?

"Yes," the King replied. "Last time I checked, you were wanted for a **crime**."

No, that wasn't it.

Theft.

Fraud?

"No . . . consorting with known magic users, that was it. Hollow, **arrest** that girl!"

There was a pause.

"Hollow's not here, your majesty," Link said.

"And my mother might not react well to you arresting me, Uncle," Priscilla added.

"ARREST HER ANYWAY," the King told his soldiers.

"No, wait," his other head said. "We can make an exception, just this once. What are you doing here, Priscilla?"

"Waiting for a cruise ship, of course," she laughed. "What else would I be doing?"

The King peered suspiciously at the equipment crates. "What's in all these boxes?"

"Nothing!" yelled Locki from inside one of the crates.

The King's two heads looked at each other.

"Nothing except my collection of talking beach towels," Priscilla said quickly.

"My lord!" Link had spotted the glass ball.

The King floated his throne past the crates to have a look. "What is that?"

Priscilla shrugged. "Looks like a wrecking ball to me."

It did look like a wrecking ball. While Priscilla was distracting the King, Cos had escaped from the straitjacket and used his spray can to paint the inside of the glass!

MAGIC SECRET UNLOCKED

While Cos was putting on the straitjacket he had taken a deep breath, making his chest as big as possible. He had also pinched the fabric at the front of the jacket, making it look tighter than it was. This had allowed him to escape quickly.

"It's huge!" the King said. "What is scheduled to be knocked down, Link?"

Link frowned. "Nothing, my lord."

Thanks to her **super strength** and loyalty to the King, Link oversaw all construction. Although in Coppertown, construction usually meant destruction. The King always sent Link when something needed to be torn apart.

Priscilla's heart was racing. "It must be left over from a previous project," she suggested.

LINK

KING'S BUILDER
SILVER CASTLE, SILVER CITY
ABILITIES: UNBREAKABLE GRIP

Inside the ball, Cos was still painting. He'd only had time to spray one side of the ball, and it was slowly spinning. Soon the unpainted side would be facing the King, and Cos would be exposed.

"Well," the King said, "just so long as the wrecking ball doesn't interfere with the **magnet**."

Priscilla's eyes widened. "Magnet?"

The King pointed at the giant block of iron. "For my **treasure hunt**," he explained. "One of my ships sank years ago, and I lost some cargo that was important. Very important. But now I've finally figured out how to find it."

"I figured it out," his other head objected. "You were sitting around scratching your—"

"Activate the magnet!" the first head commanded. The King raised his hand and blasted the iron block with magic.

The glass ball swung as the metal chains were dragged toward the magnet. The crane groaned under the strain.

Inside the equipment crate, Locki slammed against the wall with a thump. "Ouch!" he yelled.

"What was that?" the King **demanded**.

Priscilla quickly sat on the crate to stop it from sliding toward the magnet. "What was what?" she asked.

Then there was a mighty shriek overhead...

As the beam of the crane snapped...

And the giant ball fell, with Cos still trapped inside!

SINK OR SWIM

The ball **crashed** into the ocean and Cos hit the inside of the glass.

"Ow," he groaned.

The ball rolled in the waves until the side with the wooden grate faced downward, letting the water in. Then it started to **sink**.

Cos had escaped from the straitjacket, but not from the shackles around his ankles. The magnet dragged them upward, **sticking** his feet to the ceiling. Now he was hanging upside down inside the glass ball with the water rising toward his face. **This was a nightmare!**

Tucked under his wristband was a long piece of metal with a crooked point—a lock pick. Cos pulled it out and jabbed it into the shackles.

DON'T PANiC, he told himself. Fear would make his heart race, and that would make his hands shake. *Just focus on the lock.*

He felt one of the tumblers click into place. That was a good start—but the roaring water had almost reached his head.

CLiCK!

He took three quick, sharp breaths, filling his lungs with

oxygen. Then there was no more time. The murky green water swallowed his head. The world went quiet. Working blindly now, Cos kept fiddling with the shackles.

CLiCK!

Click! The lock popped open. His ankles were free. But he was still trapped in the ball, sinking deeper and deeper.

One lock down, he thought. *Two to go.*

STAY CALM!

Cos swam down to the grate and jammed the pick into one of the padlocks. Normally it would only take about ten seconds to pick a lock like this, but he'd never done it so deep underwater. The light from the surface seemed very far away. The pressure was crushing his chest. His eardrums throbbed.

Click! The first padlock came loose and floated up toward the surface, drawn away by the magnet. Cos started working on the second.

Thump! The glass ball hit the ocean floor, jolting Cos. The lock pick slipped out of his grasp. The magnet sucked it up toward the surface, out of reach.

No! Cos thought desperately. He rattled the grate, but the last padlock held it in place. He was trapped, and he was nearly out of air!

A shadow fell across him. The straitjacket had floated up to the top of the ball, drawn by the magnet. There was something metal inside!

Cos grabbed the straitjacket and **squeezed** the fabric, looking for the object. There it was—a **backup lock pick**. Nonna, his prop designer, had sewn it into the lining for him.

Cos **ripped** the fabric open with his teeth. The pick floated into his hand. He jabbed it into the lock and **wiggled** it around.

Click! The padlock popped out. Cos pushed the grill open and started swimming up to the surface.

Usually it would be **dangerous** to go up so fast. Scuba divers had to rise slowly to avoid getting sick. But Cos had no choice. He was out of air.

His lungs were bursting.

The darkness was closing in from the corners of his eyes . . .

When he was only a few feet away from the surface, something grabbed his leg.

Cos screamed. A storm of bubbles escaped from his mouth. The octopus reached up to touch his face with another tentacle . . .

Then the whole world went black.

THE KILLERS

CLANG! CLANG! CLANG! Back on the shore, more and more metal things hit the giant magnet. The swords and spears were **ripped** from the soldiers' hands—Priscilla ducked as they flew past. Soon there were dozens of weapons **stuck** to the magnet, along with two padlocks, a lock pick, a bunch of loose bolts, some coins and part of a jet ski.

Link had grabbed hold of the railing beside

the pier so she wouldn't get **dragged** into the magnetic vortex. But the railing itself was starting to shake.

"Pardon me, your majesty . . ." she began. Then the railing **snapped** off the pier.

Link flew through the air, clutching the railing, and **slammed** against the magnet. Soon she was buried under a growing mountain of pipes, crane parts and small boats.

The King paid no attention. "Where's my treasure chest?"

"It must be too far away for the magnet to reach," his other head said.

Priscilla peered anxiously into the water. No sign of Cos. He had been under for more than three minutes! She tried to remember what his record was for holding his breath. Four, maybe? But that was in shallow water. The deeper you went, the harder it was to hold your breath.

With a wave of his hand, the King switched off the magnet. The pier shook as all the metal objects fell to the ground. Link emerged from the pile, wheezing.

"We need to go down there," said one of the King's heads.

"In a submarine?" suggested the other.

"No, dimwit. That would interfere with the magnet."

They kept **arguing** as the throne floated away along the pier back toward Silver City, Link and Flex close behind. The soldiers picked up their swords and shields from the pile around the magnet and followed.

As soon as they were gone, Priscilla **jumped** off the crate and **kicked** it over, revealing Locki.

Where's Cos?

"He hasn't come up yet. Has he ever been under for this long before?"

Locki checked his watch. "Four minutes! Oh, no—we have to help him! Quick!"

Priscilla and Locki ran over to the edge of the pier. There was still no sign of Cos in the dark water. Priscilla couldn't see the glass ball, either.

Locki leaped over the rail and **plummeted** toward the ocean. Priscilla took a deep breath and followed.

The water was gloomy and cold. When Priscilla's eyes adjusted to the shadows, she could see coral, seaweed and barnacles stuck to the pylons under the pier—but no sign of Cos. The glass ball was gone, too.

The ocean floor was like an underwater forest. Strange creatures darted between huge trees of coral. Clouds of seaweed drifted over big, sharp rocks. Glowing eyes watched Priscilla from dark caves.

Locki was trying to get her attention. He pointed to something white on the seabed. Cos's straitjacket! And the shackles lay nearby.

Phew, Priscilla thought. *Cos escaped!*

BUT WHERE iS HE?

Something moved in the distance. A murky shape. Priscilla squinted at it.

Is that Cos? she wondered. She hoped so—she was running out of air.

Then a second shape appeared beside the first. They were getting closer.

Locki was saying something. He looked panicked. But Priscilla's ears were full of water, so she couldn't understand what was going on.

Then the two shapes got close enough for her to see their tails, their fins . . . and their sharp teeth.

Priscilla and Locki paddled furiously for the surface. The whales were big enough to **swallow** them both in a single **bite**. But Locki was too heavy. He couldn't swim fast enough to escape.

Her lungs **burning**, Priscilla grabbed Locki's hand and tried to pull him up. But that was even worse. Neither of them could swim one-handed.

The two giant sea creatures grew nearer.

Their hungry mouths opened wide . . .

Priscilla let go of Locki and swam up to the surface by herself. Her head **burst** out of the water under the pier, and she took a deep breath.

There were no ladders or boats nearby. The pylons were too smooth to climb. But there was another way to get out of the water. She just hoped she was **fast enough** to save Locki.

Cos wasn't the only one with a spell book. As the King's niece, Priscilla had access to the royal library.

She shouted a magical phrase in an ancient language. The words meant "I create as I speak," but they sounded like "**Abracadabra!**"

Spelldust exploded from her fingers. The magic activated the giant magnet on the pier above once more. It pulled Locki out of the water as Priscilla grabbed hold—just in time! The killer

whale's toothy jaws **snapped** shut just below Priscilla's ankle, then it **crashed** back down into the water. Locki hit the underside of the pier and stuck there, **wriggling** like a fly in a web. Priscilla held on to his legs, **dangling** above the water.

The whale peered up at them with an evil eye. Another whale surfaced beside it.

"Did you get them, Barry?" it asked.

The first whale shook its huge head.

"A talking whale!" Locki gasped.

"A talking padlock!" the second whale exclaimed.

"Don't worry, Stuart," the first whale said. "They can't stay up there forever."

"Dibs on the princess," Stuart said. "The padlock doesn't look very tasty."

"I meant the game, you fool!" Barry said. "We'll **compete** to see who gets to eat the princess."

"Oh, OK."

Both whales waggled their flippers. "Rock, paper, scissors!" they both shouted.

There was a pause.

I don't have any fingers.

Me neither.

The two whales looked up at Priscilla and Locki. "You win this round," Stuart told them. "But we'll be back."

They **disappeared** into the dark water.

"That was close," Locki said.

Priscilla turned off the magnet, and they climbed onto the top of the pier.

"We need to find Cos," she said. "But we need something to **protect us** from the whales, and I need to be able to breathe."

"I brought some scuba gear for emergencies."
Locki rummaged through an equipment crate.
"But Cos has been under for more than eight
minutes. He could be—"

"I know," Priscilla said. "But if
anyone could have **survived** that,
it's Cos."

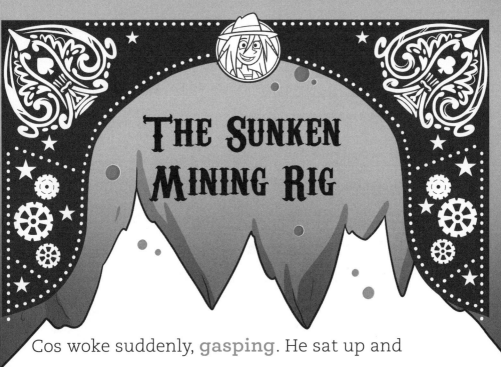

THE SUNKEN MINING RIG

Cos woke suddenly, gasping. He sat up and looked around. He was somewhere dark and cold. An underwater cave.

"Hello?" he called out.

There was no answer.

Suddenly he realized that although he could see and breathe, he was still completely submerged! He was breathing underwater! How was this possible?

He reached up to touch his face. His head was surrounded by a magical bubble of air which rippled when he touched it.

Cautiously, he climbed off the rock he had been lying on. The bubble of air moved with him, like a space helmet. This was amazing! He had spent his whole life in Coppertown—the ocean was a whole new world to explore.

He expected the magic air bubble to leave a trail of spelldust, but it didn't. Sparks of the dust kept appearing, but they vanished as soon as they touched the water.

It took Cos a minute to realize what this meant. If the water was **extinguishing** the spelldust, Hollow wouldn't be able to smell it on the surface.

I can do whatever I want down here! Cos realized. *I can do real magic, and the King will never know! I'm going to make that rock float!*

ALAKAZAM!

A grin spread across Cos's face. "Shazoom!" he shouted.

The floating rock **whooshed** out of the cave so fast that it left a shock wave. The ripples **knocked** Cos flat on his back. He giggled.

BOOM!

This was **fun**, but he needed to find Locki and Priscilla. They would be worried about him. He walked to the mouth of the cave. His body was still underwater, so he could only move slowly. But the **pressure** made his body light. It was like walking on the moon. If it weren't for his wet, heavy clothes, he would have floated up to the surface.

When Cos reached the mouth of the cave he saw that he was near the seabed, about three hundred feet downhill from the pier. Someone or something—

the octopus, maybe?—had taken him to this cave and protected him with the air bubble.

In the other direction, Cos saw a huge, dark shape—**a sunken mining rig**. It was as big as a city, covered with cranes and pipes and giant drills. Before it sank, hundreds of people must have worked on it, drawing up oil from beneath the ocean floor.

In winter, Silver City was heated by magic, but Coppertown residents weren't allowed to use that. They had tried solar power for a while, but the King's **floating palace** was like a large **cloud** in the sky, blocking out most of the sunlight. So instead the people of Coppertown used **oil burners** to heat their homes.

The oil came from several rigs along the coast. Cos didn't remember hearing about any of the rigs

sinking, at least not lately. This one looked like it had been here a long, long time.

Then Cos heard something. At first it sounded like laughter—but soon he realized it was actually someone **sobbing**.

"Hello?" he shouted again.

The sobbing got louder. Cos suddenly wondered if the sound was coming from a ghost—one of the miners who had been on board when the ship sank. **A chill ran up his spine**.

Cos looked toward the pier in the distance, but he couldn't risk swimming up to the surface. The King could still be up there. And it sounded like someone down here needed his help.

He shuffled across the seabed toward the sunken mining rig. The water was teeming with life—a little tuna was tightening the strings on

her **violin** while a remora was taking **photos** of a starfish. A young catfish was taking **videos** of itself and uploading them to the **Internet**. In a passing school, the teacher was scolding the clownfish for being **disruptive**.

kiss kiss

But the water close to the sunken rig was quiet. The nearby coral was dead, and no fish went near it. Maybe the oil had poisoned the water.

The glass ball which had nearly killed Cos lay near the rig. It must have rolled all the way here after the chains snapped.

As he got closer, he noticed something else next to the rig—something almost as big as the rig itself.

"Whoa!" he breathed. The rig hadn't just sunk, a ship had crashed into it. One of the huge boats from the royal navy. Its iron hull was partially jammed under the rig and appeared to be spotted with small holes.

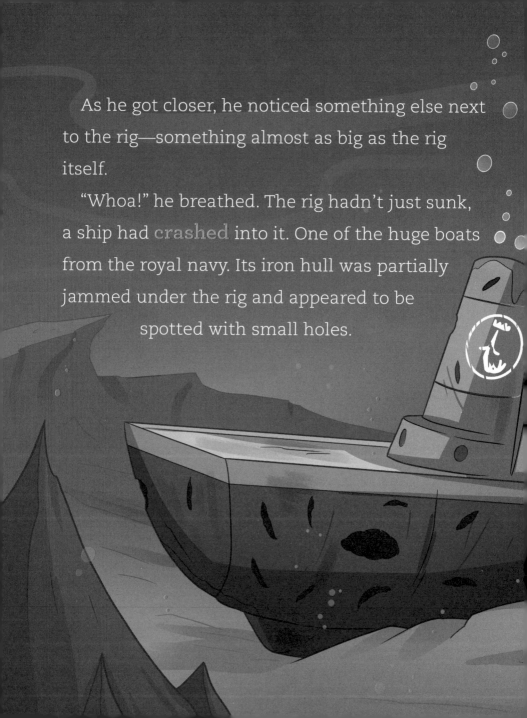

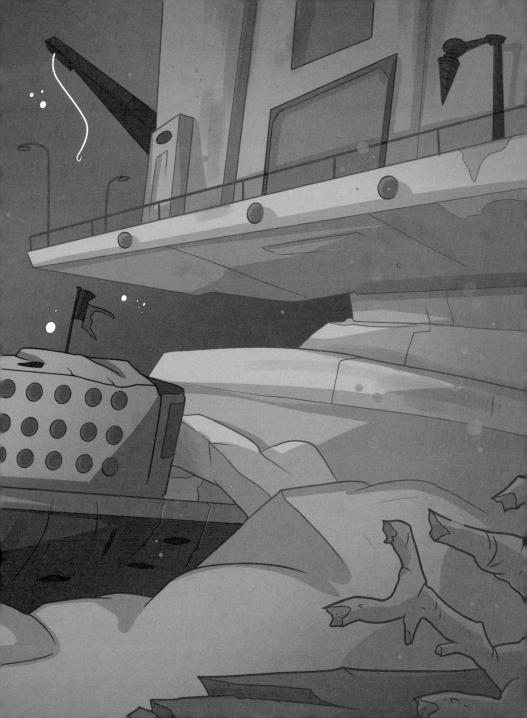

How did it crash? Cos wondered. The royal navy used magic navigation instruments that were never supposed to **fail**. But something must have gone very wrong. And what had made those holes?

When Cos reached the rig, he swam up onto the crooked platform and started moving through the narrow alleyways between the towering machines. The sobbing grew **louder**.

Cos had seen a lot of weird things. He had watched elephants **vanish** and fishbowls **appear** out of thin air. So when he turned the corner on that sunken mining rig, what he saw might not have been the **strangest** thing he'd ever seen. But it was at least in the top five.

It was a boat anchor, **weeping** next to a stack of oil drums. Every few minutes he'd wipe his nose with a tissue, but then he'd burst into tears again.

"Are you OK?" Cos asked.

The anchor **whirled around**. "Hey!" he said, quickly dabbing at his eyes. "Who are you?"

SOB!

"I'm Cosentino," Cos said. "Call me Cos. Unless you work for the King, in which case I'm . . . Paul. Paul McSmitherson."

The anchor blew his nose and **saluted**. "Captain Anchor at your service. Welcome to my rig, Cos. How did you get here?"

"That's a good question," Cos said. "I woke up in a cave with an air bubble around my head."

"Ah," Captain Anchor said. "You've met Katalin."

"Have I?"

"Yes. She's an octopus. About yay

CAPTAIN ANCHOR

CAPTAIN OF SUNKEN OIL RIG, THE OCEAN
ABILITIES: VERY HEAVY,
CRYING UNDERWATER

high." The Captain gestured. "Probably the most **magical** creature in the ocean—and certainly the only one who could do a spell like that."

KATALIN

OCEAN PROTECTOR
ABILITIES: MOST MAGICAL OCEAN CREATURE,
CAN BECOME INVISIBLE

"I nearly drowned," Cos said. "I suppose I should send her some flowers."

"You could," the Captain said, "but she'd prefer a dead crab to **munch** on, if you can find one."

Gross, Cos thought. "How did you get here?"

Captain Anchor's lip trembled. "It's a long story. You probably don't want to hear it."

Cos sat down next to Captain Anchor. "Sure I do. Maybe I can help with whatever's wrong."

"You can't. It's impossible."

"I like impossible things. What happened?"

"I loved this rig," the Captain began. "I worked here every day for a **hundred** years. The people who worked here were like family to me. Then the ship came."

"That ship?" Cos asked, pointing at the shipwreck.

"Right. It was part of the royal navy. Apparently the King's heads couldn't agree whether to go left or right, so the ship went straight ahead."

Cos might have guessed that the King was to blame. "And it **hit** your rig?"

The Captain nodded miserably. "The ship smashed into the support struts. Only some of them **broke**. We could have fixed it. But when I saw the damage to my beautiful rig, I cried and cried . . . and the tears **flooded** the place. The whole rig came down, pulling the ship with it." He hung his head. "It's all **my fault**, you see."

"It doesn't sound like it was your fault," Cos said. "You did your best."

"Yes—but my best wasn't good enough."

"What did the King do when his ship started to **sink**?"

"He jumped in the only lifeboat and sailed back to shore," the Captain said. "But I still had my emergency radio, so I called some helicopters. They got everyone off the rig before it went down."

"You **saved everybody**? That's amazing! Why didn't you escape too?" Cos asked.

"I was too heavy for the helicopters. Besides, a Captain has to go down with the ship," Captain Anchor replied. "It's maritime law. So now I spend my days walking, sitting and practicing my monologues."

Cos saw that the Captain had lined up some broken chairs in front of a shipping container, as though it was a **stage**. Some crash test dummies were propped up on the chairs.

Cos looked around at the rest of the **ruined** rig and the dark, empty patch of ocean around it. It

was the most lonely place he could imagine.

"But the Captain doesn't have to stay down with the ship," Cos said. "Why don't you swim back up to the surface?"

"I'm not a great swimmer. I was made for sinking, after all. The last time I tried to get to the surface, Barry and Stuart nearly caught me."

"Barry and Stuart?"

"Aye—two killer whales who hunt around here."

"Killer whales?!" Aside from the giant octopus, none of the fish Cos had seen here so far had been particularly big. But the water was too dark for him to see very far. The killer whales could be lurking nearby. Hopefully they were too big to squeeze between the buildings and machines on the mining rig.

"There used to be seals, sea turtles and dolphins living around here," Captain Anchor said gloomily. "Not anymore. Barry and Stuart ate them all, and now they're working their way through the smaller animals. They would have eaten me, too, except that Katalin distracted them. She made herself look like a big tasty shrimp, and then vanished when they chased her. They were confused long enough for me to swim back down to my rig."

"You're made of metal," Cos said.

BARRY AND STUART

KILLER WHALES
ABILITIES: CAN EAT ANYTHING,
HIGHLY LITERAL

"HOW COULD THEY EVEN DIGEST YOU?"

The Captain shuddered. "They probably couldn't—but that won't stop them from trying. They'll bite anything. Did you see all the holes their teeth made in the ship? They chewed the metal hull for days before giving up."

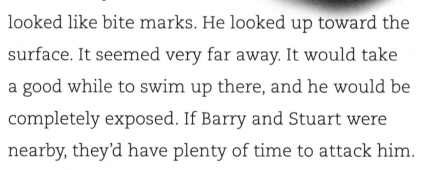

Cos remembered those holes. No wonder they had looked like bite marks. He looked up toward the surface. It seemed very far away. It would take a good while to swim up there, and he would be completely exposed. If Barry and Stuart were nearby, they'd have plenty of time to attack him.

"I'm trapped down here," the Captain said. "And I'm sorry, Cos—so are you."

TRAP SETTING

"I need to get back to my friends," Cos said. "But I can't swim faster than the killer whales."

It was an **impossible** situation. So it took Cos almost a minute to come up with a way out of it.

"I'll need a saw, a screwdriver and two wooden boxes," he announced.

"For what?" the Captain asked.

"To get us out of here. Do you have those things?"

"Well . . ." the Captain stroked his beard. "I suppose Angus might have something. Come this way."

The rig was **huge**, with hundreds of cabins and several workshops containing hoses, gas tanks, weights, hard hats, nets and more. Cos grabbed a saw from a workshop and followed the Captain to a room full of crash test dummies. They had once been used to test safety gear. The Captain said they were also useful for when he was practicing his **acting**. He had named them all, which Cos found a bit **worrying**.

"Thank you, Angus," the Captain said, pulling a tool belt off one of the dummies. He handed Cos a screwdriver. "There are boxes in the cargo bay. Oh! Good morning, Eleanor."

The Captain blushed and tipped his hat to another one of the dummies.

"Ooooookay," Cos said. "Where's the cargo bay?"

"Excuse us," the Captain told the dummies, and then he took Cos downstairs into the rig's cargo bay. It was like a big hall, with wooden crates stacked up against one wall and not much else.

"This will be perfect," Cos said.

"For what?"

"For housing **trapped killer whales.**"

Cos quickly explained his plan. The Captain didn't look convinced.

"Are you sure that will work?" he asked.

Cos was already removing the hinges from one of the wooden crates. "Sure. I've done it on stage a thousand times."

"But the audience usually isn't so close," the Captain said. "And they don't eat you if the trick goes wrong."

"You haven't met my critics," Cos grumbled. He started sawing through the underside of another crate. "Does that hatch lock?"

The Captain looked up at the hatch above their heads. "Yes. But the whales are pretty strong."

"It just has to hold them for long enough that we can swim up to the surface." Cos finished attaching the hinges and stepped back. Now one of the crates had **two lids on opposite sides**.

"It seems like a pretty simple trick," the Captain said.

"The best tricks always are," Cos said. "It's not about the method—it's about showmanship. Help me carry the crate up the ladder."

Underwater, the wooden crate wasn't very heavy. Cos and Captain Anchor hauled it out of the cargo bay without much trouble. Cos rested it on its side, next to a stack of pipes and in front of the open hatch. He opened one of the two lids.

"What about Katalin?" Cos asked. "Should we ask her to come with us?"

The Captain shook his head. "She can't breathe on the surface, and she doesn't like socializing. That's why she's invisible most of the time. Right, Katalin?"

There was a pause.

"Oh," the Captain said. "I thought she might be here. Never mind."

If Cos hadn't seen the octopus himself, he would have assumed that she was Captain Anchor's imaginary friend. "Well, all right," he said. He stood on top of the box so he would be visible.

"Let's go through the plan one more time," he said. "Then we'll do a practice run. I'll stand up here, nice and obvious. When you see the killer whales, you'll shout—"

The whales are coming!

"That's right. Then you'll hide over there, and I'll—"

"The whales are coming!" the Captain shouted again.

"Yes, that's right. Once I'm sure they've seen me, I'll jump down onto—"

"Cos!" the Captain screamed. "The whales are coming!"

Cos looked around. There they were—two huge dark shapes, swimming through the ocean toward

him. Cos hadn't realized they would be so big, and so fast. His heart kicked in his chest. It was a magician's worst nightmare—a high-stakes trick with no time to rehearse.

"Hide!" he hissed.

The Captain ducked under a nearby workbench while Cos waved his arms at the whales. "Hey!" he yelled. "Over here!"

The whales had already seen him. They swam faster, baring rows of yellow teeth.

Cos jumped down off the crate, crawled inside and closed the lid, sealing himself in.

"I saw him go in there, Barry," a voice said.

"Hey," Barry said. "Come out of the box. We have, uh . . . a present for you."

So far, the plan was working. Cos just hoped
Captain Anchor would remember his bit—

BUT THEN
SOMETHING
WENT
W
R
O
N
G.

HEADS OR TAILS

"Hey!" Locki roared. "Get away from that box!"

He was standing on the edge of the sunken mining rig, brandishing a club that he had found. Priscilla was with him, wearing the emergency scuba gear. She waved a harpoon gun menacingly at the whales. But Stuart and Barry didn't look scared.

"Hello again," Stuart said, with an evil grin.

"I'm warning you!" Locki said, waving his club.

"Bluh bluh bluh!" Priscilla added, menacingly. The scuba regulator was in her mouth, so no one could understand what she was saying.

The killer whales were probably right not to be scared. Locki's club was small, and Priscilla's harpoon gun might not even work underwater.

"Dibs on the princess!" Stuart said.

"Again?" Barry complained.

"How about heads or tails?" Stuart suggested. "You call it."

"Heads!"

Stuart flopped on the deck and stuck his tail up in the air. "Tails!" he announced. "I win!"

"How about best out of three?" Barry asked.

Stuart shook his head. "There are only two of us."

Priscilla held on to her harpoon tightly, raising it toward the whales.

"Fine," Barry said. "You eat the princess. She's got that metal thing anyway—it looks crunchy and I've got a toothache. I'll eat the softer guy in the box."

Stuart looked cross. "I've changed my mind. I want the guy in the box!"

Just then, Captain Anchor leaped out from behind the stack of pipes. "Run!" he yelled to Locki and Priscilla.

Locki stared. "A talking anchor!" he said.

Ignoring him, Captain Anchor kicked the crate over the edge into the open hatch!

Barry **dived down** into the cargo bay after the falling crate. Not to be outdone, Stuart **dived after** him.

As soon as they were in the cargo bay, Captain Anchor closed the hatch and **locked** it with a steel bolt.

"What are you doing?" Locki demanded. "Cos is trapped down there!"

"Ta-da!" Cos leaped out from behind the stack of pipes.

"Bluh?" Priscilla said.

"Oh," Locki said. "The old double-lidded box trick!"

MAGIC SECRET UNLOCKED

The whales had seen Cos enter the box through the lid on one side. While they were arguing about whom to eat first, he had slipped out through the lid on the other side and hidden behind the pipes. By the time Captain Anchor pushed the box into the cargo bay, it was already empty.

"What's that on your head?" Locki asked Cos.

Cos touched the air bubble around his head, which rippled. "A magic octopus gave it to me."

"Oh, I should have guessed," Locki said.

THUMP.
THUMP.

"The killer whales are trying to break through!" Captain Anchor said.

Locki looked at the bolt. "That won't hold them for long. Let's get out of here!"

"Wait," Cos said. "Look!"

A spotlight was sweeping across the mining rig. A throbbing engine sound made the water vibrate.

They all looked up. Something was sinking toward them from above. Something big and long, made of polished silver.

THE KING'S LOST TREASURE

Cos and his friends ran for cover. Locki and the Captain hid under the workbench, while Cos and Priscilla hid behind the stack of pipes.

But the submarine didn't come near the sunken rig. It went to the shipwreck instead.

"Bluh bluh bluh bluh bluh bluh bluh bluh bluh," Priscilla said.

Cos blinked. "Huh?"

Priscilla rolled her eyes. She took the regulator

out of her mouth and leaned in so her face was inside Cos's magic air bubble.

"The King is searching for lost treasure," she repeated. "Something went down with the ship—something very valuable. That's why he showed up with a magnet at the dock."

"What could it be?" Cos said thoughtfully. "Silver?"

Silver was the most expensive metal in Magicland, since it could be used to carry magic from one place to another—unlike copper, which could only carry boring old electricity.

Priscilla shook her head. "Silver isn't magnetic," she said. "Whatever he's looking for, we need to find it before he does."

"Why?" the Captain asked. "You don't even know what it is."

"If the King wants it," Priscilla said, "I don't want him to have it. He has too much power already." She placed the regulator back in her mouth as she moved out of the air bubble.

In the distance, the King himself emerged from the submarine. Both his heads wore diving helmets.

"But he knows what he's looking for," Locki said. "We don't. How can we find it first? It's impossible."

"**Impossible** is my middle name," Cos said.

"Your middle name is Buttercup," Locki objected.

Priscilla snorted with laughter. Cos glared at Locki.

"Cos Buttercup McSmitherson," Captain Anchor said thoughtfully.

"He's outnumbered four to one," Cos said. "We'll find the treasure first, so long as—"

Then Flex emerged
from the submarine, still
carrying his sword. He
had on a scuba mask like
Priscilla's.

Link came out next.
She was carrying a
heavy black bag—and
dragging the giant
block of iron.

Uh-oh, Cos thought.

"If they turn on the magnet," Locki whispered,
"I'll get stuck to it!"

"Not just you," Cos said. "The Captain, too!"
And the rig, he realized. And the sunken ship.
Every metal object down here would be sucked

inward. Not only would Locki and Anchor be trapped, but Cos and Priscilla would be crushed.

"We need a **distraction**," Cos said. "Fast!"

Captain Anchor stood up. "Leave that to me," he said.

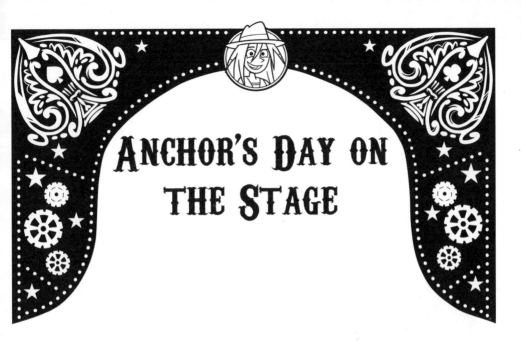

ANCHOR'S DAY ON THE STAGE

"Where's the door on this ridiculous hull?" one of the King's heads **complained**, as he walked around the sunken ship.

"They don't have—" Link began. Then she remembered that she was speaking to the King, and shut her mouth.

The King glared at her. "What was that?"

"Nothing, my lord."

"She was probably going to say," the King's other

head said, "that ships don't have doors in the hull, you nincompoop. Otherwise they would sink."

"But it sank anyway!" the first head shouted. "So who's the nincompoop now?"

"Still you, I think," the second head said.

The hull was encrusted with barnacles, and despite the bite marks, it was still solid. The glass in the portholes was **thick** and **unbreakable**. There was no way in from this side.

When he walked around to the other side of the ship, he saw a giant glass ball lying on the seabed. Half of it had been painted, so it looked like . . .

"A wrecking ball," the King said. "Hmm."

"What does that mean?" asked his other head.

"I don't know, but I know **I don't like it**," he said.

"Aha! Over here." The King's other head spotted a way into the ship. One of the portholes was smashed, creating an opening which led to the lower levels.

The King pointed at the giant block of iron. He was about to cast the spell which would turn it into a magnet, when—

"Alas, alack!" A voice rang out from the sunken mining rig. "Woe is me! What troubles I have seen!"

The King squinted at the mining rig. A ship's anchor had struck a dramatic pose on one of the towers, one hand thrown across his brow.

"Cursed, I am," the anchor continued, tears streaming down his face, "to walk these lonely depths, without so much as a mollusk for company!"

"Who is that?" the King asked Link.

The King's other head spoke up before Link could reply.

"His hat suggests that he is the captain of that rig."

"And what's he doing?"

"I believe," the King's second head said, "he's acting."

"Oh, jolly good!" The King rubbed his hands together and sat down on a rock. "I'm in the mood for a show."

"Uh, sir," Link began. "What about the treasure?"
The King waved a dismissive hand. "You search
the ship. Don't forget the bag. I'll wait here."

Grumbling, Link picked up a heavy black bag
and disappeared through the smashed porthole
into the sunken ship.

"It's working," Cos whispered.

"On the King, sure," Locki said. "But Link has gone into the ship to look for the treasure."

"You two go in after her," Cos said. "Try to **find the treasure first**. I'll stay here in case the Captain runs out of material."

"I'm as lonely as a rubber duck in an empty bathtub," Captain Anchor shouted. "As lonely as a tooth in the mouth of a really, really old shark who has lost all his teeth. As lonely as . . ."

The King wasn't the only one enjoying the show. The trio could see two **curious eyes** watching from inside some nearby coral. A tentacle waved. Katalin was here!

Leaving the Captain to his monologue, Locki and Priscilla followed Link down toward the ship. They had to crawl through a patch of **slimy black seaweed** so the King didn't see them pass.

They entered the sunken ship through the smashed porthole. The inside was dark and cramped, with narrow corridors made of rotting wood. **Everything lay on its side**—the floor was a wall, the wall was the floor.

"Watch out for Link," Locki whispered. They crept through the darkness, searching for anything that looked like treasure.

Locki gasped. Getting bent was the **worst thing** that could happen to a padlock.

Priscilla **jabbed** her harpoon gun at the piranhas, and they scattered. She patted Locki. "Bluh bluh," she said, consolingly.

Next they stumbled across a cargo hold, which looked promising at first. But there were just ropes, cannonballs and boxes of wet gunpowder.

In the next corridor they found a row of sailors' cabins. The bunk beds, closets and bathrooms were all **tiny**. Locki found it hard to believe people had lived here.

In the last cabin they found a strong wooden box with a steel frame, locked by several big padlocks.

"That must be it!" Locki whispered.

"Bluh!" Priscilla said urgently. She'd circled around to the back of the treasure chest and was looking at something behind it.

"Help me carry it," Locki said, bending his knees and grabbing the chest.

"BLUH BLUH BLUH!"

Priscilla yelled, pointing. Her eyes were **wide** and her face had gone **pale**.

"What is it?" Locki walked around to look—and

then he gasped.

Behind the treasure chest was the black bag Link had been carrying. It was open. Inside, Locki could see wires, lumpy plastic, and a timer.

IT was a

BOMB!

TRICKY ROPES

"I'm as lonely as a . . ." the Captain said. "I'm as lonely as a . . . um . . ."

"Bored now," the King announced.

"As a tomato in a fruit salad?" the Captain suggested. But it was **too late**. The King had lost interest. He was standing up, and turning back toward the sunken ship.

Cos's mind was racing. If the King went into the ship, he might find Locki and Priscilla. Even if he

didn't, he might see them trying to escape. Cos
had to distract him somehow.

He **leaped** out of his hiding place.

"That's me," Cos said cheerfully. "I suppose you'll be wanting to arrest me. But I can be a **slippery character.** You'd better tie me up!"

Cos produced three lengths of rope and held them up. He always carried them around with him, just in case someone asked him to do a trick.

Flex was already swimming over, mighty paws outstretched. He looked **strong** enough to **crush** Cos with his bare hands.

"I have three pieces of rope, all the same length," Cos said calmly. "They should be strong enough to **hold me**."

As Flex was about to grab Cos, Cos handed him one of the pieces of rope instead. He held out his wrists so Flex could tie them together.

Flex tried—but somehow the rope was **much shorter** than it had been a second ago. It wasn't long enough to go around Cos's wrists.

The big rabbit stared down at the tiny rope, confused.

"Oh, I'm sorry," Cos said. "How did that happen?"

He snatched the short rope out of Flex's grip and added it to the two longer ones in his other hand. Then he stretched the three ropes—and they became the same length, just like before.

"There you go," he said, offering Flex one of the ropes. Flex took it—but suddenly it was way too short again.

The rabbit scratched his big head.

"USE YOUR SWORD, YOU FOOL!" THE KiNG YELLED.

Flex raised his sword—

And then Link burst out of the sunken ship.

"I've PLANTED THE BOMB! We gotta go!"

Cos and Captain Anchor looked at each other. "Bomb?" Cos said.

"Of course! I nearly forgot," the King said. "Come on, Flex! Here, boy!"

Forgetting all about Cos, Flex dog-paddled toward the submarine.

The King, Flex and Link all piled into the submarine. The hatch closed, and the gleaming vessel cruised away like an alien spaceship.

Locki and Priscilla burst out of the ship.

"Guys!" Locki cried. "There's a bomb in the ship! They weren't trying to recover the treasure—they wanted to blow it up!"

Cos was already swimming as fast as he could—toward the ship.

"What are you doing?" Locki demanded. "Swim away from the bomb!"

"We have to save the treasure!" Cos yelled.

"You don't even know what it is!"

But Cos was already inside the ship.

THE BOMB

Cos turned around and around, looking for the treasure.

Priscilla swam in after him. "Bluh bluh," she said, pointing.

Cos followed her into the room with the treasure chest and the bomb. He **dragged** the chest toward the door. It was surprisingly light, but it wouldn't fit through the doorway. Someone must have put it in with magic.

Cos checked the timer on the bomb.

It was **too late** to save the treasure—and it was too late to save himself. He would **never** get away in time.

Cos looked around, **panicking**. There was nothing he could use.

Locki and Anchor ran in. "Cos! We have to get out of here!"

"There's no time," Cos said. "Look!"

"Bluh!" Priscilla looked like she had an idea. She was moving her hands around her head and pointing to Cos.

"What is it?" Cos asked.

"She's acting!" Captain Anchor said wisely.

Priscilla kept moving her hands **urgently**, making a shape around her head like a—

"Like a magic air bubble!" Cos shouted. Suddenly he knew exactly what Priscilla had in mind.

Leaving the treasure chest in the cabin, he scooped up the bomb and ran out of the room, through the winding corridors of the sunken ship. The timer **ticked down and down**. The bomb seemed to vibrate in his hands. It was like it was excited about going off.

Cos burst out of the ship, emerging right next to the glass ball from his failed escape attempt. He looked around at the dark ocean.

Nothing happened. As Locki, Priscilla and
Captain Anchor emerged from the sunken ship,
Cos swam over to the coral reef, where he had
seen Katalin watching the Captain's show.

"Katalin!" he cried.

"She's not here," Captain Anchor said.

Cos ignored him. "Katalin, please! We need you!"

Still nothing—then the ground blinked.

"Thank goodness you're here," Cos said. "Can you make another air bubble? A bigger one?"

The octopus looked **quizzically** at him.

The timer only had thirty seconds left.

"Inside the glass ball," Cos said. "So it floats back up to the surface. **Hurry!**"

The octopus shrugged with four of its eight shoulders and pointed a tentacle at the glass ball. Suddenly the ball was full of air. A haze of spelldust glittered around it, each spark vanishing as it touched the water.

Immediately the ball lifted off the ocean floor and started to rise toward the distant surface.

The grate Cos had escaped through was still open. Before the ball was out of reach, Cos let go of the bomb and cast a spell of his own.

SHAZOOM!

Cos shouted the spell as he thrust both hands forward in the water.

Pushed by Cos's magic, the bomb flew through the open grate and landed inside the glass ball!

The ball carried the bomb up, up, up toward the surface. There were only a few seconds left on the timer.

"EVERYONE TAKE COVER!"

Cos yelled.

Everyone swam back toward the ship. Locki and Anchor dragged themselves through the smashed porthole. Priscilla and Katalin followed. Cos was last. He was about to squeeze through, when—

High above them, the explosion vaporized
a huge sphere of water, sending a shockwave
straight down. The sunken rig shuddered and
began to break apart, sending debris floating in
every direction. The force threw Cos against the

hull of the ship. The seabed shook. There was a deafening crash as the ocean churned around them. The powerful currents cracked the ship in half like an egg.

And then, silence.

Cos sat up, groggy. Cracked rocks and broken parts of the mining rig lay all around him, along with scattered hard hats and crash test dummies.

But he wasn't hurt. The glass ball had taken the bomb far enough away. This had been his narrowest escape so far. If only there had been an audience to share it with.

"Is everyone OK?" he called out.

Everyone said yes, except Priscilla, who said "bluh" as she and Katalin emerged from the ship. Katalin waved a tentacle to put a magic bubble around Priscilla's head so she could spit out the regulator and talk properly.

"Finally," Priscilla said. "I was getting pretty sick of that."

Cos's eyes settled on the treasure chest, which lay between the two halves of the broken ship.

It looked unharmed.

"Let's get this up to the surface," he said. "I want to see what the King was so desperate to destroy."

"The rig is my home," the Captain said, gazing mournfully at what was left of it.

"The rig was your home, when all your friends lived on it," Cos said. "Now your friends are up on the surface."

The Captain looked tempted. "But I'm an anchor," he said finally. "I belong at the bottom of the sea."

"You're an actor," Locki said. "You belong on the stage. And we're building a brand-new theater you could use."

For the first time in decades, Captain Anchor smiled. "Really?"

"Just wait until you see it," Cos said.

He turned around to say goodbye to Katalin, the octopus who had saved his life twice now—and he saw that her eyes were wide with terror.

"What is it?" Cos asked.

Katalin pointed with all eight tentacles.

Everyone turned around—and saw the two killer whales looming right behind them!

BARRY AND STUART

Barry and Stuart grinned. Enormous mouths glinted with pointy teeth.

Barry was hungry. *This time I'll get them!* he thought.

"Run!" screamed the human called Cos. The princess and the two metal things swam back toward the broken ship, while Cos headed toward the remains of the mining rig.

"Where's the octopus gone?" Barry asked,

looking around. She had turned invisible again.

"Who cares? Look at those juicy humans!" Stuart gloated.

"Lost your harpoon have you, Princess?" Barry yelled, as he chased Priscilla. He stretched open his jaws to bite her, but she zipped through a porthole.

"You'll keep," Barry snarled. "Like tuna in a can!"

Stuart was already **chasing** the other human, Cos, who was still swimming toward the rig, but he was too slow. Stuart would catch him in no time.

Silly human, Barry thought. He raced after Stuart. Maybe they could go halvsies.

Cos was **dodging junk** from the shattered mining rig as he swam through a patch of seaweed. As he fled, he scooped up a floating hard hat and put it on his head. The whales didn't know what he was doing, but they didn't care. A hard hat couldn't save him now. They had almost caught up to him.

And then they both realized that Cos had vanished.

The two whales turned around and around. "Where did he go?" Barry demanded.

"He must be **hiding in the seaweed**," Stuart said.

It was true. There was nowhere else he could be hiding. The two whales circled, peering down into the forest of seaweed.

After a minute, the human must have thought they were gone. He sat up.

Barry almost didn't see him. Cos's dark clothes and black hair would have made for **excellent camouflage,** if not for the bright-yellow hard hat on his head.

Barry didn't give him another chance to escape.

He opened his mouth wide and swallowed Cos whole.

EATEN ALIVE

"No!" Locki cried, watching through a broken porthole.

"Cos!" Priscilla shouted.

"Mr. McSmitherson!" Captain Anchor wailed.

The two whales were arguing now.

"I said halvsies!" one yelled.

The other burped. "And I said no."

They started slapping each other with their flippers. Now was the perfect chance for Locki,

Priscilla and the Captain to escape—but none of them moved.

"What do we do?" Locki hissed. "How long can a person survive inside a whale?"

"Not long," Cos said.

"Then we have to hurry," Locki said. "Let's—hey! Cos!"

They all whirled around. Cos was missing his hard hat, but otherwise he looked fine. He certainly didn't look like he'd just been swallowed by a killer whale.

"But how?" Captain Anchor asked.

"A magician never tells," Cos said. "Let's just say that seaweed makes a surprisingly good wig, and that I hope the whale likes the taste of crash test dummy."

Anchor gasped. "Eleanor!"

The two whales were still **fighting**. "What are we waiting for?" Locki whispered. "Let's get out of here!"

Priscilla was already strapping her air tank to the treasure chest. "**Rocket propulsion**," she explained.

Cos realized what she meant. "Everybody hang on!" he said.

They all grabbed hold of the chest, and then Priscilla unscrewed the valve on her air tank. **Bubbles exploded out** of the tank, and the chest shot upward like a rocket, with everyone clinging to the sides!

The whales looked up as the chest blasted past. "Hey!" one shouted. "They're getting away!"

But the killer whales couldn't keep up.

The treasure chest **burst out of the water**. The magical bubbles around Cos's and Priscilla's heads popped.

They **skimmed across the water** like a jet ski toward the shore. They were coming in way too fast. The chest hit the sand with a **thump**. Priscilla, Locki, Cos and the Captain all went flying.

"Is everyone OK?" Cos asked.

Priscilla nodded.

Locki coughed up some sand. "I'm OK," he said.

Captain Anchor was hopping up and down with excitement. "Look at all this!" he said. "Sun! Sand! Seagulls! There's so much I'd forgotten."

Cos patted him on the back. "Welcome home,"
he said. "Let's see what's inside this treasure
chest!"

As Locki got to work on the padlocks, Cos
wondered what they would find inside. Silver?
Weapons? Stolen art?

The locks popped open, and the lid rose up.

A book?

Cos picked the book up, and gasped. It was a copy of **The Encyclopedia of Magic**—the same book he had hidden in his attic. There were hundreds of spells inside. "I don't understand," the Captain said.

"My uncle doesn't like anyone but him to have any magical power," Priscilla explained.

"Wait." The Captain looked alarmed. "The King is your uncle?"

Locki looked around nervously. The King's soldiers patrolled this beach every few hours. "Where are we going to hide it?" he asked.

"Why hide it?" Cos asked. "Let's do what we always do: bring magic to the people."

Later that day . . .

A girl walked into the Coppertown Library looking for something new.

One of the books caught her eye. It seemed to have a slight sparkle. As she picked it up, her eyes widened. This was a book of spells! She had seen nothing like that since the evil King banned magic. With some reading and a bit of practice, the world would be at her fingertips.

The girl looked both ways, in case it was a trap. But still no one was here. She tucked the book into her bag, and hurried home.

Quiet in the
Library

You can learn Cos's trick from page 148!

ROPE TRICK TRiO
MAGiC TRiCK iNSTRUCTiONS

REQUIRED ITEMS:

3 ropes of different lengths (e.g., 24 in., 16 in., 8 in.)

METHOD:

1. Show three different lengths of rope (FiG. 1).

FiG. 1

2. Hold them in your left hand, first the shortest, next the medium and then the longest (FiG. 2).

FiG. 2

3. Bring up the bottom end of the short rope and place it next to the top end of the long rope between your fingers and thumb (FiG. 3). Secretly cross the top end of the long rope over the bottom end of the short rope. Bring up the bottom ends of the two remaining ropes (FiG. 4).

FiG. 3

FiG. 4

4. Using your right hand, take the three ends on the right, as shown. It will appear that each hand has an end of each of the three ropes (FiG. 5).

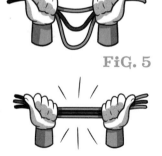

FiG. 5

FiG. 6

5. Give a sharp tug to the ropes. They will become equal in length (FiG. 6).

187

6. A loop between the short and long rope is hidden in your left palm (**FiG. 7 and 8**).

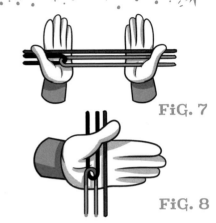

FiG. 7

FiG. 8

7. Drop the ropes from your right hand. Hold the "loop" carefully in your left hand and use your right thumb and first finger to take away the "single" rope. Count it as "one" (**FiG. 9 and 10**).

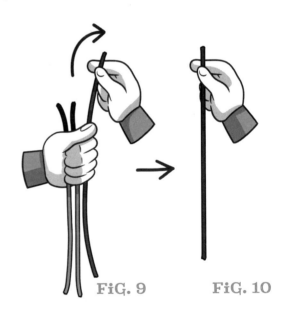

FiG. 9

FiG. 10

8. Return the "single" rope and secretly exchange it for the two looped ropes, counting them as "two" (FiG. 11, 12 AND 13).

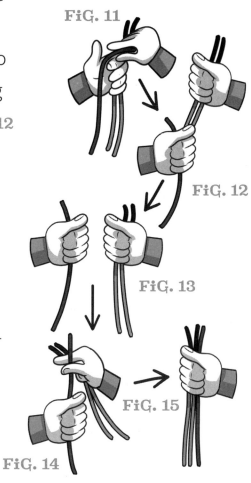

FiG. 11

FiG. 12

FiG. 13

9. Take the "single" rope from your left hand, adding it to the other ropes. Count as "three." It appears as if each rope was shown separately (FiG. 14 AND 15).

FiG. 15

FiG. 14

10. Put all of the ropes into one hand (FiG. 16).

FiG. 16

11. Pull them out one at a time to show the spectator they have returned to their former lengths (FiG. 17).

FiG. 17

TA-DA!

COSENTINO is now regarded as one of the world's leading magicians and escape artists. He is a multiple winner of the prestigious Merlin Award (the Oscar for international magicians) and is the highest-selling live act in his home country, Australia.

Cosentino's four prime-time TV specials have aired in over 40 countries and he has toured his award-winning live shows to full houses across the world.

JACK HEATH is a bestselling, award-winning Australian author of thrillers and used to be a street magician!

JAMES HART is an Australian children's illustrator who has illustrated many books.

Photo credit: Pierre Baroni

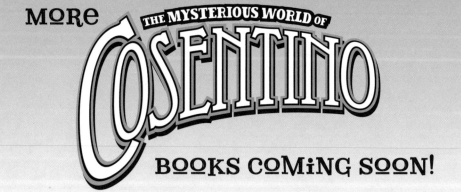

MORE **THE MYSTERIOUS WORLD OF COSENTINO** BOOKS COMING SOON!